DISCOVER SERIES
COCINA

Licuadora

Abrelatas

Rallador de Queso

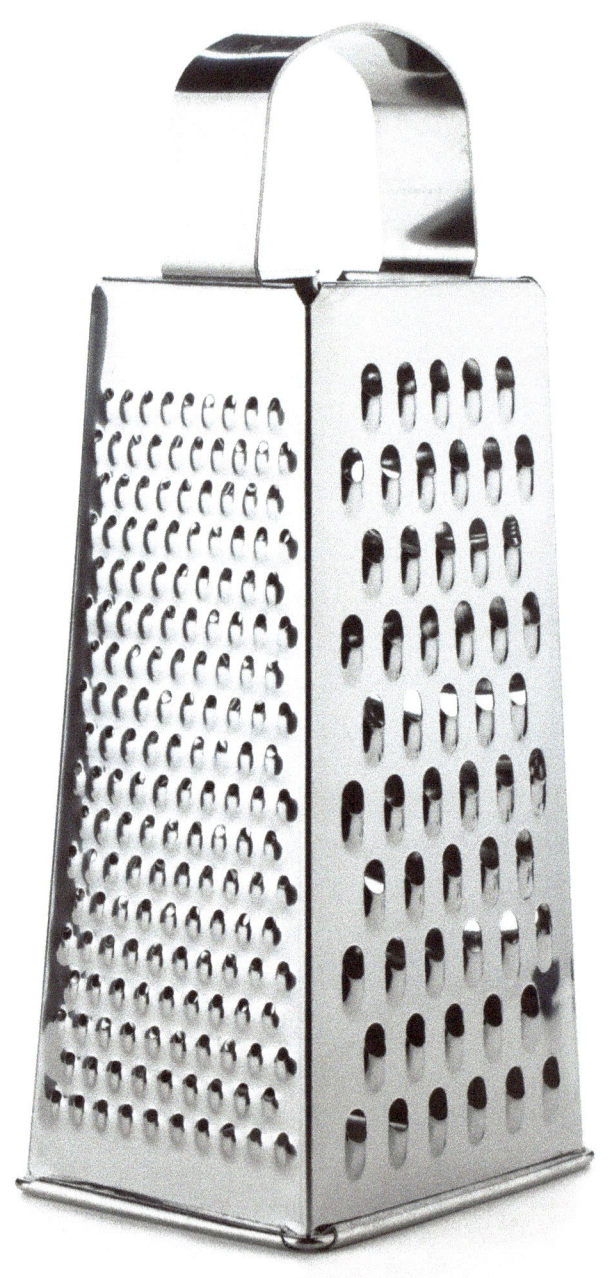

Palillos

Tazas de Café

Utensilios de Cocina

Jabon para Trastes

Lavaplatos

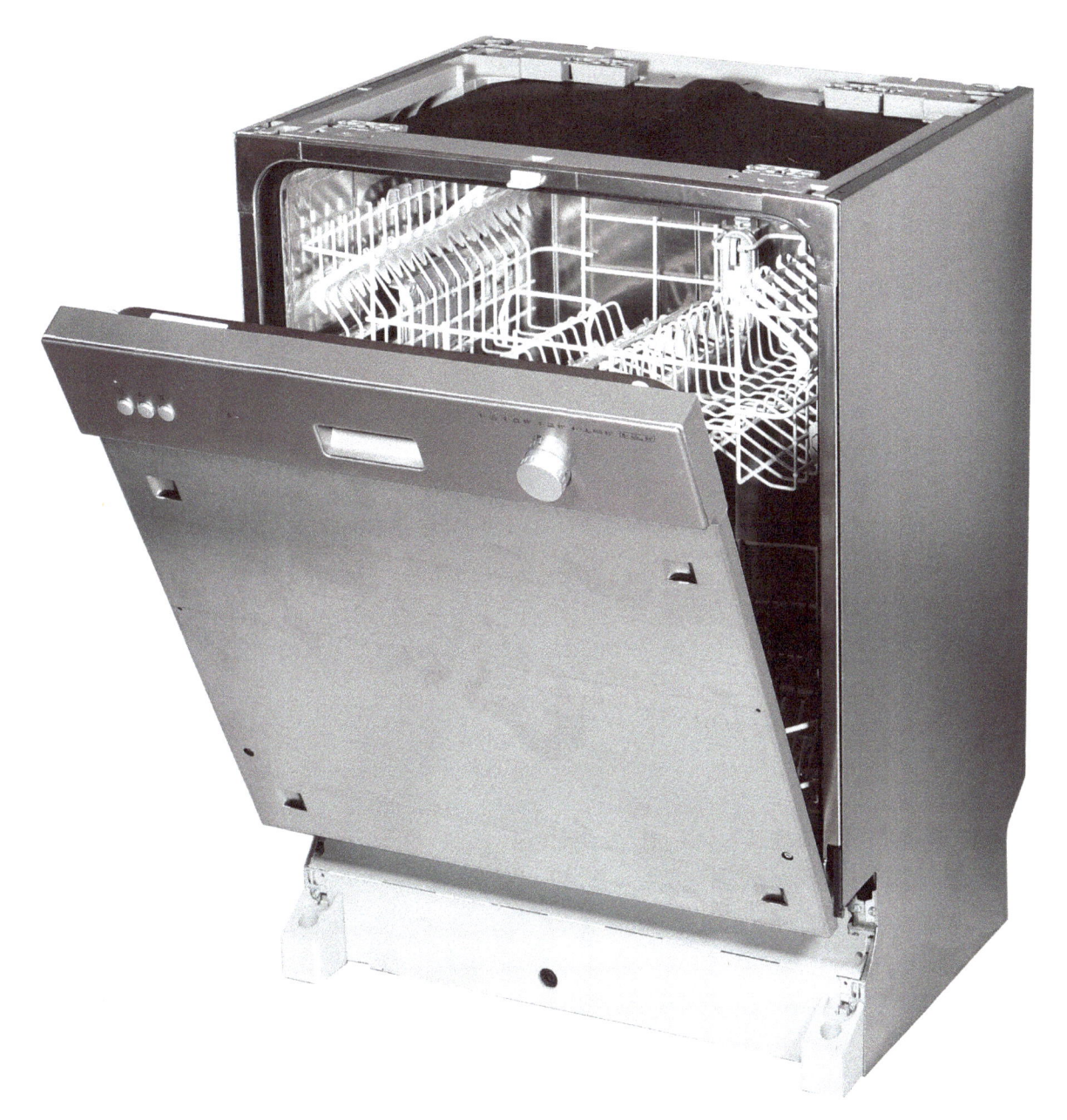

Hervidor Eléctrico

Procesador de Alimentos

Tenedor, Cuchara y Cuchillo

Sarten

Cuchillo de Cocina

Peso de Cocina

Microondas

Aceite de Olivo

Contenedores de Plástico

Ollas y Sartenes

Refrigerador

Olla Arrocera

Rodillo

Ensaladera

Salero

Tostadora

Jarra de Agua

Make Sure to Check Out the Other Discover Series Books from Xist Publishing:

Published in the United States by Xist Publishing
www.xistpublishing.com
PO Box 61593 Irvine, CA 92602

© 2018 by Xist Publishing All rights reserved
Translated by Victor Santana
No portion of this book may be reproduced without express permission of the publisher
All images licensed from Fotolia
First Spanish Edition

ISBN: 978-1-5324-0701-7   eISBN: 978-1-5324-0702-4

x*ist Publishing

www.ingramcontent.com/pod-product-compliance
Lightning Source LLC
LaVergne TN
LVHW070950070426
835507LV00030B/3477